Little Rat Makes Music

MONIKA BANG-CAMPBELL

Illustrated by MOLLY BANG

HARCOURT, INC.

Orlando   Austin   New York   San Diego   Toronto   London

www.HarcourtBooks.com

Library of Congress Cataloging-in-Publication Data
Bang-Campbell, Monika.
Little Rat makes music/Monika Bang-Campbell; illustrated by Molly Bang.
p.   cm.
Summary: Little Rat loves the violin but hates to practice, until her teacher
suggests she perform a duet with one of the advanced students at the holiday concert.
[1. Violin—Fiction.   2. Music—Fiction.   3. Concerts—Fiction.   4. Rats—Fiction.]
I. Bang, Molly, ill. II. Title.
PZ7.B2218Lf   2007
[E]—dc22   2005027536
ISBN 978-0-15-205305-5

First edition
H G F E D C B A

Printed in Singapore

The illustrations in this book were done in
pencil, gouache, and watercolor,
with some chalk dust, on illustration board.
The display type was set in Elroy.
The text type was set in Adobe Garamond.
Color separations by SC Graphic Singapore
Printed and bound by Tien Wah Press, Singapore
Production supervision by Christine Witnik
Designed by Brad Barrett

To Muffy

—M. B.-C.

*To Daddy Rat, the most
patient accompanist
in the world*

—M. B.

Chapter 1

Little Rat's family was very musical.
Daddy Rat could play the drums.
He could play the piano.
He could even play the xylophone
and the glockenspiel.
He had played them all in band
when he was young.
Mama Rat loved listening to music.
She loved to sing, too.
She frequently sang in the grocery
store. She ALWAYS
sang in the bathtub.

Little Rat's parents took her to concerts.
Mama Rat took her to folk-music concerts
at the Community Hall.
Little Rat got to clap her hands and sing along.
Daddy Rat took her to fancy concerts in the city,
where they listened to huge orchestras.

Little Rat loved watching the violinists.
They played all sorts of notes.
They played deep singing notes
and fast plucking notes.
They played really high notes.
They played low, gentle notes like whispers.
The violins shimmered in the bright lights.
The seats in the auditorium were red velvet
and very soft.
Little Rat was enchanted.

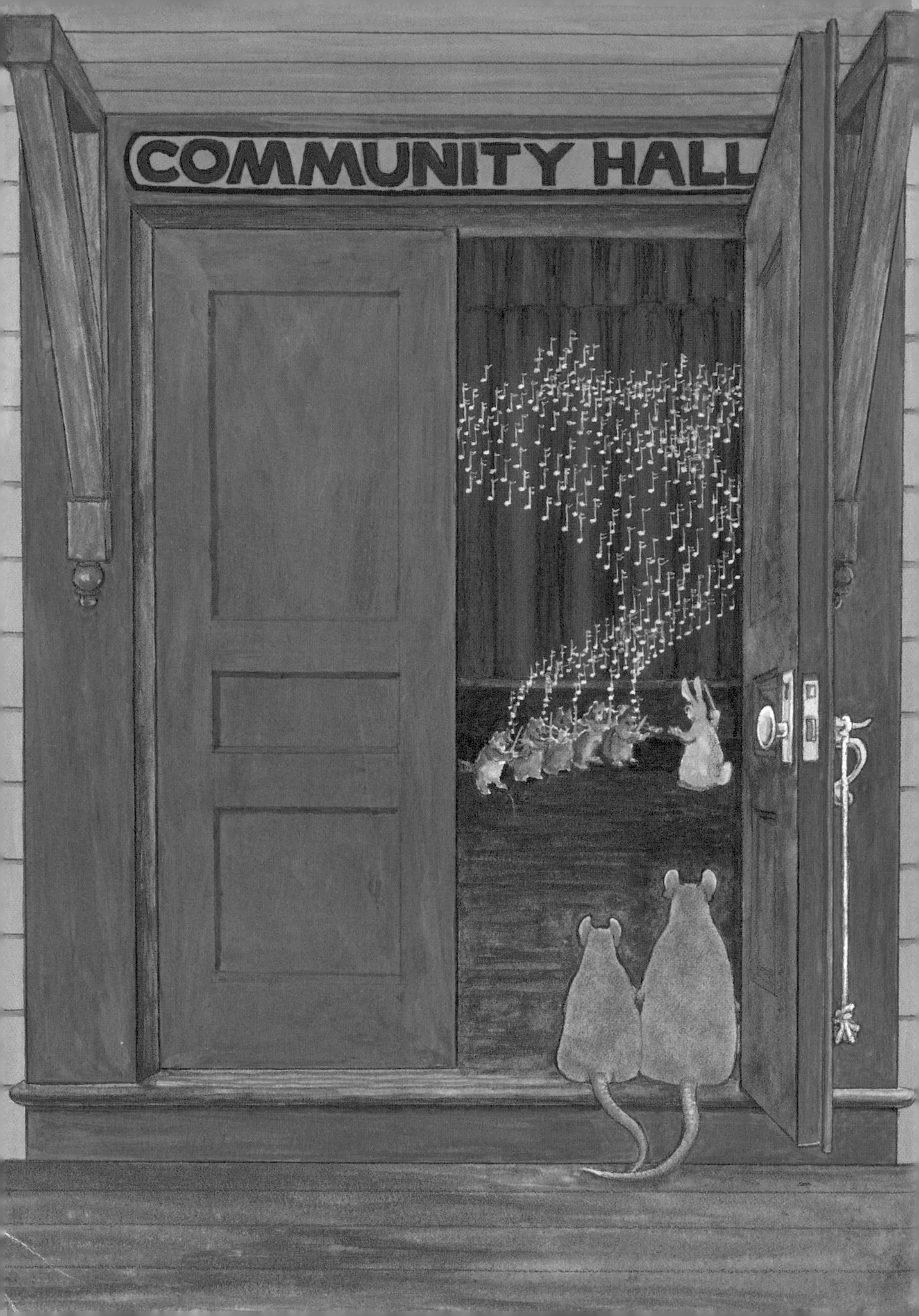
COMMUNITY HALL

Chapter 2

Every Friday after school,
Little Rat and her mama would take a walk
around the pond.
One afternoon, they heard beautiful music
coming from the Community Hall.
"Let's stop and listen," said Little Rat.
They climbed the stairs.
Mama Rat opened the door.
Little Rat's eyes grew wide.
The music was coming from youngsters
like Little Rat, all playing tiny violins.
Little Rat and her mama listened for a long time.
Mama Rat whispered,
"How would you like to make music like that?"
Little Rat said only one word:
"Awesome!"

Chapter 3

At her first violin lesson Little Rat was excited,
but nervous.
She had never even held a violin before.
Luckily, she was not alone.
She chatted with the other students
while they waited for the lesson to begin.
Suddenly, the teacher, Miss Wingbutton,
stomped into the room.
"SILENCE!" she shouted.
This surprised everyone.
They did not expect to be yelled at.
Miss Wingbutton was short,
just like her temper.
She had little tolerance for silliness.
"Good afternoon!" she said.
"Is everyone ready to learn the violin?"
"Yes," the students squeaked.
"Then let's get started."

Carefully, Miss Wingbutton took
her violin out of its case.
She asked everyone to copy what she did.
"When you are not playing,"
Miss Wingbutton said, "hang the bow on
your right index finger, like this."
The students copied her.
"When you are ready to play," she said,
"lift the violin up to your shoulder
and hold it under your chin."
Once more, the students copied her.

Little Rat was getting bored.
She wanted to play music
like she'd heard at the concerts.
How hard could it be?
She started sawing back and forth on the strings.
"Stop that!" Miss Wingbutton yelled.
Little Rat's heart jumped.
She lowered her bow.

On the way home, Mama Rat asked,
"What did you think of your first lesson?"
"It was no fun," said Little Rat.
"Miss Wingbutton was scary.
We didn't learn to play a song.
We didn't even get to play a note.
I want to play songs *now*."

At home that week, Little Rat practiced
how to take her violin out of its case.
She practiced how to hold her bow.
She practiced how to hold her violin.
But practicing wasn't much fun.
Little Rat thought it was BORING.
I should switch to playing the drums, she thought.
All I'd have to do is bang the drums with sticks.
Little Rat daydreamed about marching
in a band.

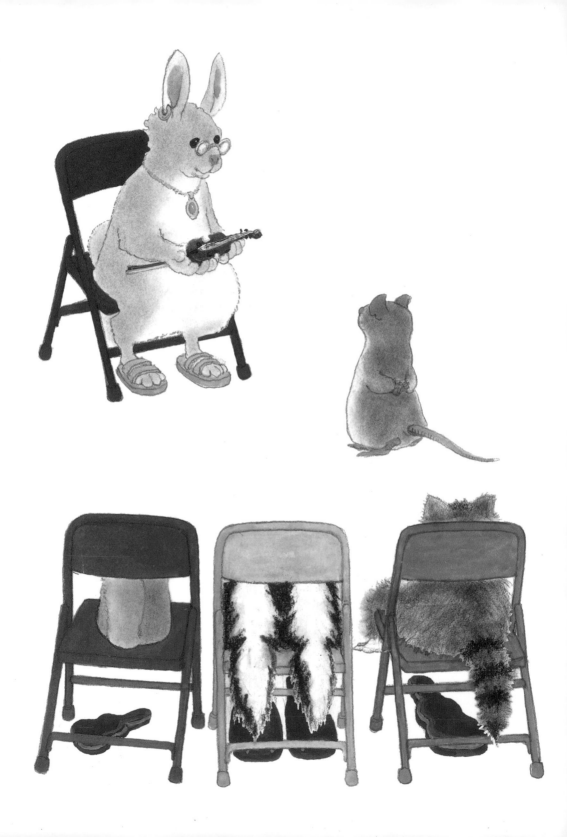

Chapter 4

At the next lesson,
Miss Wingbutton placed small strips of tape
on the fingerboards of each violin.
"These are markers," she said.
"The markers show you where to put
your fingers to make the right notes.
Moving the bow across the strings
is called bowing.
Bowing plus pressing the strings
makes music."
That sounds EASY! thought Little Rat.
"Now you will each play a note,"
said Miss Wingbutton.
"Little Rat, please go first."

This was the moment
Little Rat had been waiting for.
Her mind filled with the glorious sounds
that would float from her violin.
She placed her bow on the A string.
Miss Wingbutton said,
"One and two and ready . . . play."
Little Rat pushed her bow down hard.
She drew it across the string.

SQWAAAAAAKK!

What was that? wondered Little Rat.

It sounded like an angry seagull.

"My goodness, Little Rat!" said Miss Wingbutton.

"That was a very powerful first note!"

Little Rat was triumphant.

She had made a very powerful first note.

Chapter 5

Little Rat went to her violin lesson every week.
The students started to learn whole songs.
Miss Wingbutton asked them
to memorize their songs before each lesson.
Little Rat liked her lessons.
Little Rat liked playing the violin.
But Little Rat did NOT like to practice.
Little Rat was supposed to practice
every day for half an hour,
but getting herself to do it was like
wrestling a goat.

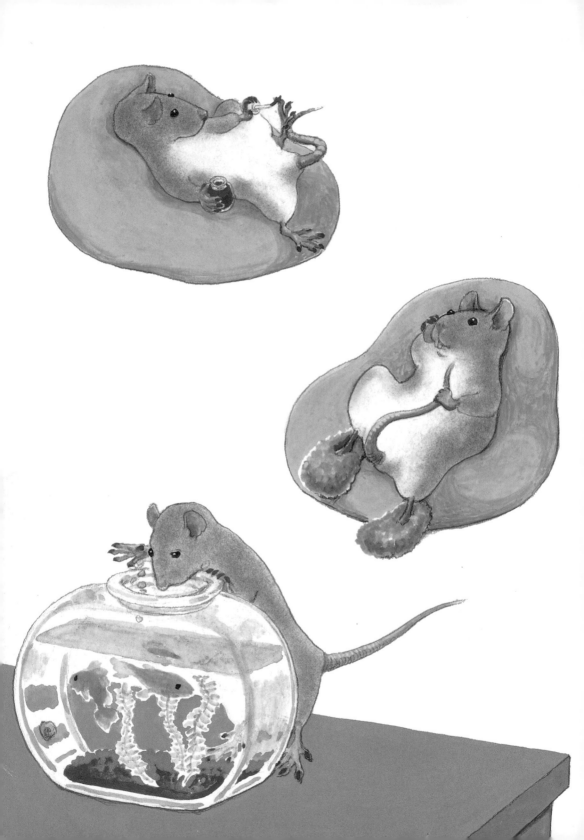

She could always find something
more entertaining to do.
She painted her toenails.
She talked on the phone with her friends.
She took care of her pets.
Even cleaning the litter box was better
than practicing.

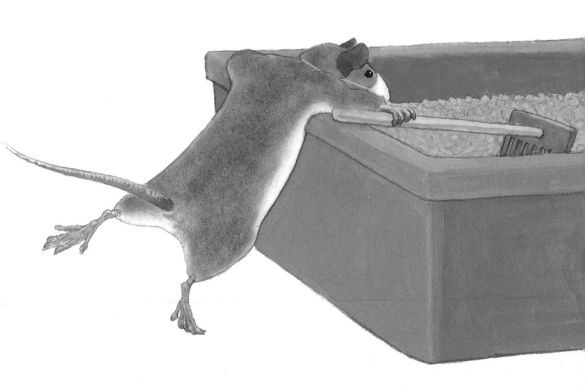

Daddy Rat tried to help.
"Let's go work on the song now," he said.
"I'll play along with you on the piano."
They played together for a few minutes
until Little Rat hit her first wrong note . . .
and her second . . .
and her third.

Little Rat's fur stood on end.
She felt a violin-practice tantrum coming on.
"THIS IS STUPID!" she bellowed.
Then she marched off to her room
and slammed the door.

Little Rat sat on her bed steaming.
She heard a knock at the door.
"Come in!" she barked.
Mama Rat sat down next to her.
"It sounds like you are
pretty frustrated, Little Rat," she said.
"I can never get it right," Little Rat grumbled.
"When I play it wrong over and over,
I feel like I am going to explode."
"I know it is difficult," said Mama Rat,
"but yelling and slamming doors does not help.
No more tantrums.
Tantrums are not music.
They hurt our ears."

Chapter 6

Miss Wingbutton knew Little Rat hated to practice.
She also heard the beautiful tone
Little Rat produced from her violin.
She thought Kitty,
one of the advanced students,
might be able to help.
Little Rat started going to Kitty's house
once a week after school.
Kitty was a very patient tutor.
And practicing with her was a lot more fun.
When Little Rat made mistakes,
Kitty would joke.
"I think Mozart would have liked that variation,"
she'd say. "Now let's play the one he wrote."
Then she would help Little Rat get it right.

Sometimes Kitty would
pretend she was a composer.
She would swoop the bow across her violin
and talk in funny voices.
One day, Kitty imitated a conductor
she had played for.
She climbed up on a stool.
She flapped her arms and did a hula dance.
Kitty looked so silly that
Little Rat burst out laughing.
Little Rat laughed so hard she farted.
Her ears turned bright pink from embarrassment.
Then she looked at Kitty.
"Not one of my nicest notes," she said.
Little Rat and Kitty
both fell on the floor
laughing.

Chapter 7

Little Rat still did not put
much effort into practicing,
but she did love her weekly lesson with Kitty.
This gave Miss Wingbutton an idea.
At Little Rat's next lesson,
Miss Wingbutton asked,
"How would you like to play a duet with Kitty
at the holiday concert?"
Little Rat was so shocked
she almost dropped her bow.
How could she possibly play well enough
to perform with Kitty?
"It's going to take a lot of practice,"
said Miss Wingbutton.
"Are you ready to put in that much effort?"

Little Rat went home and thought.

I will have to memorize the whole piece perfectly.

I will have to keep my violin from squawking.

But my violin squawks a lot. . . .

I do not want Miss Wingbutton to get mad at me.

I do not want to disappoint Kitty.

And I do not want to embarrass myself.

Little Rat looked down at her little pink fingers.

"I am going to do it," she said out loud.

"And I am going to do it the best I can."

Little Rat began to practice very hard.

Daddy Rat helped her every night after dinner.

This did not mean there were no more tantrums,

but there were fewer than before.

Little Rat and Kitty practiced their piece
over and over.
Little Rat still made a lot of mistakes.
"Playing music is like eating
a big pile of spaghetti," said Kitty.
"You can only eat one bite at a time
or it makes a big mess.
Let's eat this bite today."
So they practiced part by part.
A few weeks before the concert,
Little Rat played the piece for Miss Wingbutton.
"I can hear that you have
practiced very hard, Little Rat," she said.
"It sounds to me like you are ready."

Chapter 8

The Community Hall was decorated
with little white lights and candles.
The smell of pine needles filled the air.
Little Rat thought it was magical.
She wasn't as nervous as she expected to be.
I'm just going to do the best I can,
she said to herself.

Little Rat and Kitty took the stage.
The lights dimmed.
They began to play.
Little Rat remembered all the notes.
But more than that,
she played the notes with feeling.
Little Rat had never done *that* before.
For the first time, she heard beautiful music
coming from her violin.
It sang like she had dreamed of
when she had first started playing.
She felt like one of the violinists
at the concerts in the city.

Before Little Rat knew it,
she and Kitty had finished their piece.
The audience was standing up and clapping.
Little Rat and Kitty bowed.
Kitty gave Little Rat a big hug.
"You did it!" Kitty whispered. "That was awesome!"
Miss Wingbutton gave Little Rat a nod of approval.
Little Rat thought she might have even smiled.

At home, Little Rat and her parents celebrated
with cake and ice cream.
It was late.
Little Rat yawned and said good night.
She went to her room and put on her jammies.

She looked at her violin.
She walked over to it.
She picked it up and began to play.
Not for Kitty,
not for Miss Wingbutton,
and not for practice.
Little Rat played because she wanted to.

And for the second time that night,
she made beautiful music.